My Own Big Bed

JONNO

by **Anna Grossnickle Hines**
pictures by **Mary Watson**

Greenwillow Books New York

For Jacob
—A. G. H.

For Grace and Sarah Jane
—M. W.

Gouache paints were used to prepare the full-color art.
The text type is Della Robbia BT.
Text copyright © 1998 by Anna Grossnickle Hines
Illustrations copyright © 1998 by Mary Watson
Greenwillow Books, a division of William Morrow & Company, Inc.,
1350 Avenue of the Americas, New York, NY 10019.
www.williammorrow.com
Printed in Hong Kong by South China Printing Company (1988) Ltd.
First Edition   10   9   8   7   6   5   4   3

Library of Congress Cataloging-in-Publication Data
Hines, Anna Grossnickle
My own big bed / by Anna Grossnickle Hines;
pictures by Mary Watson.
   p.   cm.
Summary: A child proudly shows off her very own
brand new big bed while also telling herself that she
can deal with fears about sleeping in it for the first time.
ISBN 0-688-15599-5 (trade).   ISBN 0-688-15600-2 (lib. bdg.)
[1. Beds—Fiction.   2.Fear—Fiction   3. Bedtime—Fiction.]
I. Watson, Mary, (date) ill.   II. Title.   PZ7.H572My
1998   [E]—dc21   97-34476   CIP   AC

I have a brand new bed—
a brand new *big* bed just for me!
Tonight I'm going to sleep
in my own big bed.

I can get in, and I can get out—
in and out all by myself.

What if I fall out?

I can fix that.

In my own big bed I can put my arms out
as wide as they go and reach down with
my toes.
I can stretch and stretch and not touch anything,
not anything at all.
What if I get lonely?

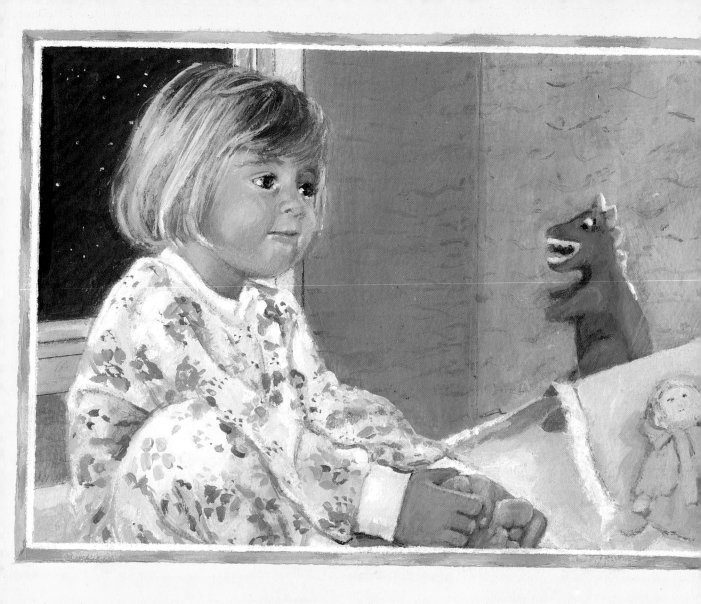

I can fix that.

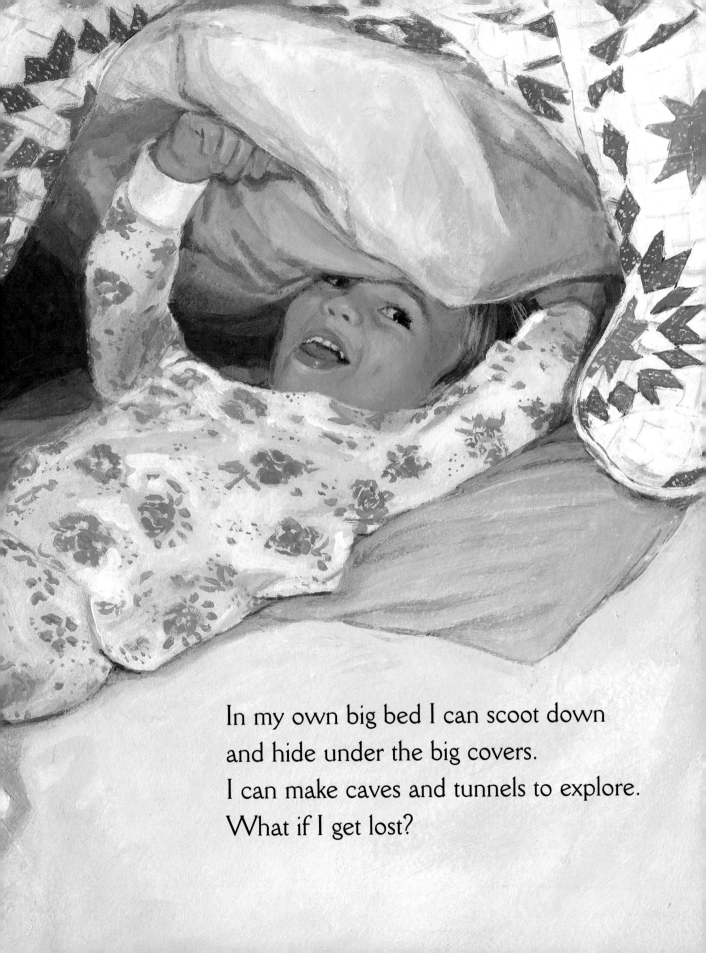

In my own big bed I can scoot down
and hide under the big covers.
I can make caves and tunnels to explore.
What if I get lost?

I can fix that.

I won't get lost under my *little* blanket.

In my own big bed I can see all around
with no bars in the way—no bars to keep me in,
no bars to keep other things out.
What if I get scared?

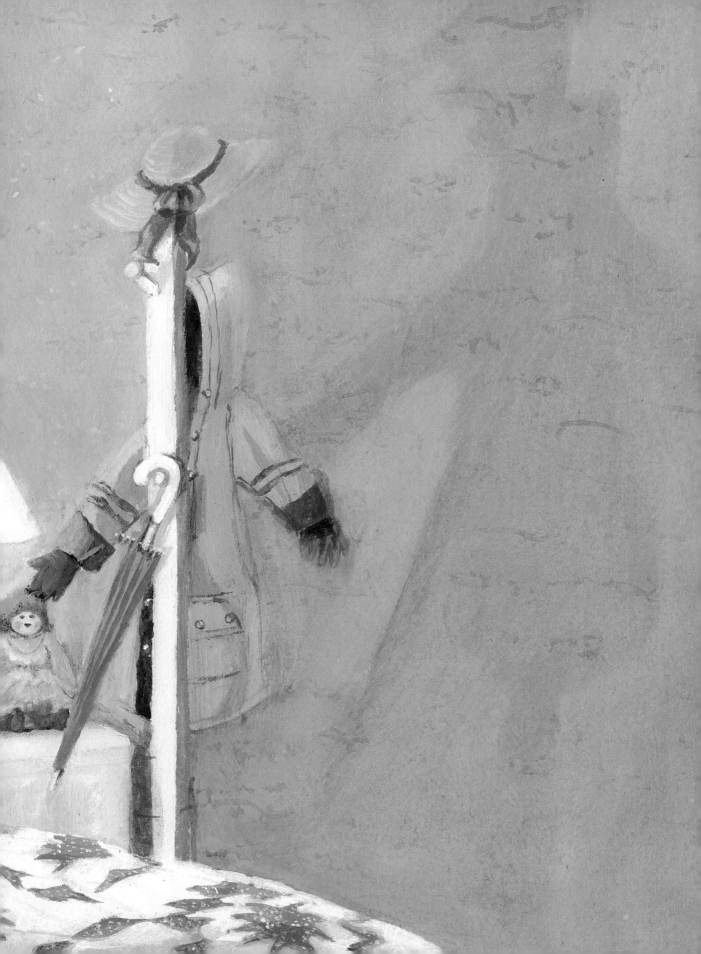

Can I fix that?
I could sleep in my little bed with the bars.
But I don't want to.
I want to sleep in my big bed.

Can I fix it if I take my great big bear?
If I take my great big bear
and my ferocious dragon?
Yes, I can. I can fix it so I won't be scared.

In my own big bed Daddy can sit beside me
to read my bedtime stories.

Mommy can tuck me in and kiss both cheeks
and nuzzle my nose.

Now I'm snug
and cozy
and safe
and sleepy
in my own big bed.